AF499337

Connor

The Guardian Angels Pack

Volume 1

Virginie T

Translated by Feriel Benhamiche

Legal deposit: April 2020

Prologue

Originally, the world was populated by humans, shapeshifters and fatels. Apparently, there was peace between peoples even if we mingled very little, living next to each other without real contact and all had a well defined place. But if we had scratched the surface, we would have discovered that the reality was quite different.

The fatels had held power for decades. Normal, their ranks included prophetesses, telepaths, telekinesists and other creatures with extraordinary power. They were very powerful and acted as judges in case of conflict because of their exemplary wisdom. Certain shapeshifters clans envied this power. They considered themselves just as powerful and, as predators, felt that it was up to them to rule the world. They wanted to be the powerful chiefs, unlike the fatels who ruled with rightness and empathy. And the packs had an undeniable advantage: the animals felt the magic which circulated in the blood of the fatels. The

Black pack, among others, was one of those clans in search of wealth and recognition.

With method and patience, the dissident clans exterminated one by one all the fatels to reach the high economic and political spheres. The first affected were the prophetesses. The clans wanted to eliminate in priority those who had the capacity to predict their project, and therefore attack them. Most humans ignored their physical particularity, because these, very precious for their people, lived almost with self—sufficient. But shapeshifters knew all about them. They had no offensive power and their eyes betrayed them in the face of enemies. Impossible for them to hide among humans. Despite their incredible power, they could not do anything against the massive attack that hit them. The others were then tracked down and killed one by one in the penumbra, without that it raise any questions. Car accidents, heart attacks or attacks of "wild animals" in the forest. Nothing seemingly suspicious, even if it has raised questions among humans and shapeshifters over time. The rebels made them disappear from the face of the Earth and the existence of the fatels quickly fell into oblivion. Since there was no concrete evidence pointing to the culprits, only suspicion, no one was punished.

No one has avenged this peaceful people exterminated for their essence. A real genocide. For our salvation, the rebel packs did not become the world masters either. Humans and other packs realized what had happened under their eyes and were horrified by their own inaction. Things have changed, evolved, since this drama, by strengthen ties between humans and shapeshifters, so that such a tragedy can never happen again. But it was too late: the damage was done, the magic people had been wiped out.

Actually, this is what everyone has thought for the past twenty—five years ...

Chapter 1

Sevana

I do my shift at Jefferson Hospital as I do five days a week, two to three times a day. I love this place. I work in the intensive care unit of a small hospital in the center of a town mainly directed by humans, a people of which I am one. I know I am useful here, and that is why I chose this position six years ago. I want to help people and this is the perfect place to do it.

— Hello Sevana. Did you have a good weekend?

— Hello Ashley. Not bad and you ?

— Great. A nice weekend to stay in bed with my new lover. Did you have interesting meetings on your side?

Always the same question on Monday morning. It’s boring and a little exasperating. I love Ashley. She’s been my friend since I was hired in this department, however I know exactly what her raised eyebrow means. My sentimental life, or rather, the absence of my sentimental life, has been his favorite topic of discussion for as long as I can remember. I'm only twenty—six, damn it! I don't feel the panic of my biological clock that seems to worry my friend so much. To believe that I have an expiration date and that I will soon expire! Not that I'm not interested in men. I have had relationships before. Let's just say that my little peculiarity is not to everyone's taste and that few have given me enough self—confidence to show them my real self. Not to mention my extraordinary ability which sometimes teaches me things that I would prefer to ignore and which aborts my flirting much sooner than expected. Like, I'm just a hobby before Mister's next real adventure. It doesn't really make you want to stay with the said oaf who just wants to have a good time with me. I don't want to be a quick date by the way. I'm better than that. That's why I know in advance that my weekend activities will not be to Ashley's liking.

— No. I had a cocooning Sunday with a good book and a hot bath. A real relaxing weekend.

— You are despairing. At this rate, you will end up being an old maid and you will live surrounded by cats! When are you finally going to find yourself a nice little human to take care of you?

I stick my tongue out like a kid. What she may think or fear is going over my head. I am sure that when the time is right, the man made for me will come into my life and never leave it.

— Do we meet to eat?

— Okay. See you later.

Why do I agree to join her for the meal each time? I know how the conversation will turn out. She will still try to arrange a meeting with one of her acquaintances. And these arranged meetings, for the few that I accepted just that she leaves me a little quiet, they all turned out to be disastrous. Men around her tend to imagine that I only think about sleeping or that it's all cooked, since after all, I'm lucky that they pay me a little attention, and so they don't have to make an effort to seduce me.

I go into the nearest room, internally blaming my weakness in front of my friend, I just don't want to offend her, but it costs me. I mentally shake myself to put aside my thoughts and take up a professional position. I go to the patient's bedside and perform my ritual. Always the same: I read the file, check the patient's constants and touch his hand. This last point is my personal trademark. There is only me who do it this way and I remain extremely discreet about this detail, but it is essential. Let's say that I have, um, intuition. Sometimes, with a simple physical contact, I learn things about the person in question. I see her future, a possibility, what she could be if no outside person intervenes, anyway. As part of my work, I will know whether the patient's condition will deteriorate or not. In service, I'm called the Guardian Angel. I have saved many lives over the years and my colleagues are no longer surprised when I ask for help for a patient who seems stable. As now, for this wolf shape—shifter who arrived very badly this morning, and whose heart will stop beating in a few moments. I'm not wasting time and activate the intercom.

— RESUSCITATION'S TROLLEY ROOM 4.

The doctor on duty came running, followed by my friend Ashley, who was responsible of the floor in pairs with me.

— Check-up, nurse Slat?

— Male wolf shapeshifter patient, 20 years old, multiple lacerations in the abdomen, several broken ribs, double fracture in the left arm.

— Reason for the alert?

— Imminent drop in heartbeat.

The doctor does not question my diagnosis. I regularly depend on his team, he is used to my alerts given several precious minutes in advance and if, at the beginning, my alerts were called into question, this is no longer the case today. The doctors trust me completely. He immediately prepares the defibrillator and everyone waits in silence to intervene at the right time. We are not going to electrocute a man whose heart beats at a regular rate. I am sure of my prognosis, but one thing puzzles me: it is not the first shapeshifter that I deal with, even if it is rather rare to receive them in this hospital, and I know that their metabolism differs of humans. They usually heal quickly. Much faster than us. but, this man is as damaged as when he was admitted. None of these wounds have started to heal and he has not regained consciousness once. Something is missing. An anomaly that I cannot identify and that seems important, and the presence of a trace of bite in his neck worries me. I'll be doing a thorough search later. Maybe his blood test will tell me more about him. For now, no time to wonder any longer about this anomaly. The heart sensor starts to slow down.

— We are losing him, let's move away.

The doctor performs the first electric shock without

any results.

— We increase the power.

Another shock followed by manual pulmonary ventilation by me while Ashley takes care of the resuscitation device.

— Again.

At the third discharge, the patient finally stabilizes. His heart curve takes regular peaks. A new discreet physical contact on his hand allows me to confirm that he is out of danger. For the moment, anyway. Only the future will tell us if he is finally saved. I will keep an eye on him closely until the first sign of awakening and then I will stand back, keeping the promise made to my parents.

— Another great job, Miss Slat. Someday you'll have to explain to me how you're doing to predict the aggravation of patient health when there is nothing indicates to us. You allow us to do miracles. You saved the life of this canine. It would be very helpful to have more nurses like you.

I smile at him blushing and shrugging my shoulders because I have no answer for him. I do not know how my talent works and I have long considered it as a malediction, because I have no control over it. I have always had this ability, as far back as my memory goes, and my parents forbade me to talk about it to anyone. They have been very clear on this point. Interdict to talk about this and my physical imperfection, because people would instantly reject me. My family had a precept: people do not like those who are different,to blend into the masses. I followed their advice and it has been pretty successful so far.

That's when two men appear in the room. Very imposing, broad with shoulders and a muscular body, they hardly pass in the frame of the door and are impressive. Their faces are closed and their eyes glisten with reflections of molten gold. shapeshifters, without a doubt. I've never seen them in excellent physical shape and the malevolence that they give off makes me uncomfortable. I take a step back to find myself in a dark corner of the room. Probably useless reaction, because they scrutinize only the man lying under the sheet, without more interest for the people around.

— Tsss, tsss, tsssss, why did you resuscitate him? We will have to do the job again now. This time, we will not leave until we are sure of the success of our mission.

Repeat what? What mission? Their facial expression may be neutral, but their intentions seem bad.

Ashley immediately stands in front of them, hiding their view of the wolf. She barely reaches them at shoulder level, but you shouldn't trust her frail body, my friend can be fierce if necessary.

— Sorry gentlemen, visits are prohibited in this area. Are you family?

Without even giving her a look, the more hefty of the two, a long haired brown, a gash on the cheek, gives her a violent blow on the head. I scream when I see my friend falls to the ground like an inert mass, blood on her temple, unfortunately drawing all their attention to me. They then approach me with a flexible but threatening approach. Real predators and I became their prey. I understand better why my parents taught me to stay away from animorphs. My supervisor courageously tries to intervene despite an undeniable difference in size. My colleague looks like an unlucky hobbit against two orcas! There is a clear imbalance of forces. Unfortunately for him, the second man grabs him by the neck and makes him tumble against the wall at the other end of the room without any difficulty, as if he weighed no more than a feather, making him losing consciousness. So I find myself alone facing them and in all lucidity, I do not make the weight against these two brutes with doubtful intentions. From my height of sixty centimeters and fifty poor kilos, I certainly do not have the strength to push back males who seem so swollen with steroids that their veins stick out on their biceps. I have to not to lose time while I wait for the guards to arrive.

My shout must have raised the alarm and the reinforcements should not be long in coming. I absolutely must make them speak. I can do that. When I stress, I talk nonstop, a real blabbermouth. The only problem, I am beyond stress, I am rather terrified, which ties my throat instead of untie my tongue.

— What do you want ? I can certainly help you.

— Just to resolve a clan business. Nothing that concerns you, doll. Stay quiet and you'll only get a small bump on your head. You are of no interest to us and you should not try to save this traitor again.

Ashley's aggressor looks at his accomplice, indicating with a head movement the inanimate and defenseless patient on his hospital bed, giving him a silent command. I want to intervene, but Mister scar blocks my way by placing himself on my path without taking my eyes off, blocking my visibility on the patient. I have to tilt my head to the side to observe the sequence of events. The one I suppose to be the underling goes towards the patient and plunges his hand directly into the thorax of the wolf without hesitating for a second, as if everything was normal, clutching what must be his heart until the outline of the electrocardiogram is flat. The distress beep is deafening in my ears and a cry of terror sticks in the back of my throat in the face of the horror of the situation. I am there, helpless, attending a real execution. Once satisfied with the work of his partner, Mr. Muscle stares at me again and takes a deep breath to smell my perfume, smell is an essential sensc for them. I know it's a shapeshifter's reflex, which doesn't prevent me from being uncomfortable, as if someone had touched me without asking my permission. His eyes suddenly widen and he grunts as he rolls up his lips, discovering long, sharp fangs. That's a bad sign. It seems that the scent of my soap displeases him. I stammer more than I speak.

— Sorry, my perfume is a little strong.

— Fatel, you shouldn't exist. I will solve this problem immediately. My ancestors didn't do it all for nothing. The fight is not over.

What is he talking about ? He is crazy. The fatels have indeed disappeared. I learned this during my history lessons when I was a child, without knowing under what circumstances. The fatels are invoked only for the scientific advances they have allowed. It is not a very glorious story, and both humans and shapeshifters prefer to ignore their inaction and the consequences on the world that this has engendered. I was only a baby when the last fatel was massacred and my parents are all human. Trying to understand his intention to kill me, although his reason eludes me, I try to dodge towards the door, but he grabs my arm with incredible force. My bone creaks in a terrible noise, but I don't have time to scream my pain when sharp claws like razor blades pierce the flanks to hold me against his chest. He then plunges his nose into my hair and inhales again.

— You smell magic. It's going to be a real delight. Don't move, it'll be fast. Or almost.

That's when the second man, thinner, but just as athletic, sniffed my neck before planting his fangs deeply.

— How is it possible ? I thought this people have disappeared.

— And it is the case because she will join them into nothingness.

— As soon as we take what we want?

— Of course. The strength tenfold is for us.

Please no. They won't settle for a bump at the end. A huge ball of anxiety clogs my larynx. They cut my stomach, bite my collarbone several times, sucking my blood like vampires, except that they are only fiction and my aggression is real. It looks like they are enjoying torturing me. I feel my strength give up as my blood spills over the white tiles, forming a most macabre contrast, and the suffering is unbearable. I pray that I will pass out before my last breath and that my ordeal will end, which happens when armed guards open the door with a crash to rescue me.

Chapter 2

Connor

I take my coffee on the terrace of my chalet, like every morning, when I can. I often travel for work and I have made this place my haven of peace. The exterior is all wood, from floor to roof, and arranged to receive the entire pack, with tables and chairs scattered here and there at the front of the building. The place is quiet, in the middle of a wood, ideal for the metaphor cheetah that I am. Impossible to guess, seen from here, the original function of this place. I need greenery and space to feel free and relaxed and congeners for social contact. It is for this last reason that my chalet is not isolated in the middle of nowhere as I sometimes feel the urge, but near other chalets of the same style as mine, without being on top of each other, giving us some privacy.

I hear activity coming from the surroundings, doors slamming and leaf creaking under the weight of the walkers. My lieutenants, as well as my beta, will soon come to see me for our daily ritual: racing and fighting in our animal form. Sometimes dominant members of the pack join us to keep themselves good form. This is important for team cohesion and essential for strengthening the pack bond. After all, we are an extraordinary clan. The only pack of animorphs of different species. I love these moments of calm when we give free rein to our animal part.

— The form, Connor?

— Not bad and you ?

— Hum, like a morning when I wake up alone in my big bed.

Phew, Nate is incorrigible. If he sleeps alone, without a woman to warm his sheets, he is in bad mood. However, here, the rules are strict and the same for everyone: no foreigner (man or woman) in this specific case, on our territory. It’s a security matter. This territory is a refuge for many of us and it is impossible to enter it without being authorized. And since we haven't been out for many days, since the end of our last mission in fact, Nate is starting to feel alone.

— We'll go out tonight, if you want. You can find to yourself a hot bear.

— Nop, not a bear, they are too insistent. Each time they expect a serious story and it is no way. I prefer to wait for the right one, the only one created for me.I understand Nate's point of view. As shapeshifters, we know that we have a soul mate somewhcrc on this carth. Unfortunately, few find it and it is not uncommon for a shapeshifter to decide to unite with another who is not intended for him, but who makes him happy. I am like Nate. I'm waiting for the perfect woman for me. I am convinced that if I deserve it, fate will put her in my way. My beta arrives at that time and takes the conversation along the way.

— Like all of us bro. Right Connor?

— Exact. Hi Sean. The others arrive?

— Liam and Owen spent the evening in town. You know them, they surely have a hard time getting out of bed of their conquest of the day. They shouldn't be long.

Yep, that remains to be seen. They must still sober up.

— OK, let's start girls.

I love to tease them, it motivates them. In reality, they are formidable fighters, as seasoned as I and loyal friends. I would put my life in their hands without hesitation. We undress quickly so as not to disintegrate our clothes and take the shape of our animal. My beast is pleased to be on all fours and does not waste time, it leaps on the lion in front of us, which responds with a stroke of the paw much wider than its own. It is much larger than us, but my animal is more agile and faster. Everyone has their assets. Sean and I turn around, mutually seeking a flaw in the defense of the opponent, when Nate's bear charges us and sends us rolling against a tree. His favorite technique: the ball of demolition. Nate is not delicate, but he is effective. Grrr, I'm going to have a bump. He's going to pay me this big oaf. Against a grizzly bear, the smartest thing is to run to get it tired. A mastodon weighing more than three hundred kilos is formidable when it loads, but it certainly does not have the endurance of my feline. My animal is the fastest in the world, I am unbeatable in racing. I still have time to get started. So I go between two trees when the bangs of bone characteristic of a shapeshifter sound. The latecomers have finally had to get out of their ethylic coma and don't waste time getting into the dance. The game will get tough. A huge gray wolf hits me on the right flank just before I pick up speed while a beautiful black panther, as graceful as deceitful, grabs my left hind paw to make me fall to the side. Liam and Owen are used to work in pairs and have their own attack techniques. Fortunately, my buddy is over two meters tall. Nate jumps and drops heavily on Liam who moans under the weight. The bear is really not in finesse, I am pleased not to be its target when I see a gray crepe buried by a hairy mountain of a bright brown. I take this opportunity to grab Owen by the skin of the neck and force him to back away. Sean then launches into the fray, roaring and growling. To all of us, we form a huge ball of yellow, black, brown and gray fur, speckled in places. Difficult to distinguish who claws who or what. We fight, bite and run most of the morning before taking human form in front of my chalet, covered with tufts of hair, blood and saliva. For a stranger, the scene we offer could be alarming. In reality, our injuries are superficial, the goal of the exercise not being to badly injure , but to acquire new techniques and new reflexes as well as to improve our skills in the art of combat. In few hours, nothing will appear there. I grab the jet of water and rinse us unceremoniously. We are not afraid of cold anyway. Our blood is warmer than that of humans, protecting us from temperature variations. We then sit outside with a beer to take stock of the training.

— Good job guys. Liam, Owen, was the night short?

— Sorry Connor, but this chick was too sexy and ...

— I don't need details,Owen thank you. You were less efficient, slower than usual. Force is not everything in the case of an attack. Watch out.

I sometimes show myself hard, but our survival depends on it. And I care about each of these dumbass, even if I would never confess to them.

— Relax Connor, we don't have a mission right now.

Ah, Nate’s optimism. In the group he is the quiet force and the defender of the oppressed. As if these guys need to be defended.

— I know Nate, but it won't last, it never will.

Sean doesn't say a word, he knows I'm right. He is my beta, my right arm, and manages the secondary missions when I am not available. He takes even less good time than me and I already take few. And just like for me, this job is his whole life and his reason for existing on this earth. He is the one who brought us together, even though we all have personal reasons for being here. The five of us represent the little Guardian Angels pack. There are other members of course, but we are the most important and the strongest. I'm the chief, the alpha. I am responsible for everyone and I take this role very seriously. The last three present with me are the defenders, the lieutenants. They have a role just as essential as me. Without the five of us, no more packs. It would become vulnerable and quickly disappear. Our work, thanks to substantial subsidies, allows us to support the clan and has given us this territory, an ancient, highly fortified human military base. But this is valid only if we stay alive to do the job. Our job is not without danger. We serve the governor when the human police are overwhelmed by events. Only for witness protection in investigations involving shapeshifters. Humans are no match for an angry and determined animorph. What are fists worth against claws and fangs that can shred you in less than a second? So we're fighting ours to make justice prevail, replacing the missing fatels. We are the most powerful species on earth and I estimate, like my companions, that this does not put us above the law. Still, the witnesses must be alive to appear in court, and this is where my team comes in. Most of the people we have saved, often from their own pack, some alphas who love excess and oppression, have settled here with us. This is how this pack was born.

Chapter 3

Connor

Well, what did I just say to Nate? To believe that I am clairvoyant, or that the governor heard me. I knew it had been too long since my phone rang.

— Hello Governor. How are you ?

— Good, but truce of banality. We have a problem.

As usual, he would not call me otherwise. His phone calls are never to announce good news. But his tone makes me nervous and puts my senses on alert. The governor is never worried. Tense, stressed, yes, but never anxious and today I could almost smell his fear through the handset. My friends immediately notice my change in posture, I stiffened, my instincts alert, and immediately take their seriousness, awaiting information about their next mission.

— I'm listening to you.

— There was an assault in a human hospital. A wolf who had been admitted the same morning was killed.

It's rather unusual for an animorph to end up in the hospital, especially a human hospital, but apart from that ...

— OK, but I can't do anything for him anymore.

— Obviously, and an investigation is underway to find out the reasons for his pitiful state when he arrived. But you could help a nurse who was at his bedside.

— Of course. Did she know him? What pack is she in?

— To my knowledge, she did not know the victim and she does not belong to any pack. She's a human and she's in a coma. She was attacked by the shapeshifters who came to finish off the wolf.

I get up from my seat and start pacing. This story is not trivial.

— I'm sorry ? Usually, clans don't even tire of threatening humans because they are too scared of retaliation to testify against them, so attack them! We've only protected shapeshifters until today. Why do they hurt this human woman?

— This is what you are going to have to find out while protecting her. They ran away and left her for dead only because of the guards arrived in the room with handguns . They were forced to shoot several times so that the animorphs decided to drop their victim. Vigils who have spotted several shapeshifters on guard around the human hospital since the assault on Miss Slat a week ago.We think that they want to know if she is alive or if she will succumb to her injuries soon. And they might want to finish the job when they find out that she survived. It is out of the question that a war breaks out between humans and shapeshifters. Humans will not disappear without a fight if the matter gets out.

— Okay. Send me the address. We'll be leaving within an hour.

This is a strange case. She will be the first human to benefit from our protection. Not that it is not important, I respect everyone's life, human or shapeshifter, it is the same for me. Everyone has a place on earth and a role to play. Why would shapeshifters want the death of a nurse? How important is it to want to make sure that she is dead, at the risk of starting a war? It does not mean anything.

— Connor, a problem?

— I don't know, Sean. This mission is unusual. We have to protect a human left for dead by shapeshifters.

— Why would a clan do this?

— This is the hundred thousand dollar question that will have to be answered. The governor fears a war between the two peoples. Which could happen if a pack attacks a human hospital. We may be physically stronger, but we are not invincible. Humans may be afraid and shoot at all of the surrounding animorphs. Sean, I entrust the pack to you. The others, we take off in an hour.

I take my bag in my room without wasting time, turning and returning events in my head without understanding the meaning.The trip to the hospital took us 3 hours by plane plus thirty minutes by car. Have you ever seen wild animals on a plane? It's like putting a lion in a cage. It's not good. We are not made to fly. So we arrive anxious at the hospital , nervous and a little aggressive. We would need to release the animals to relieve the pressure. Unfortunately, the shapeshifters I see watching without any discretion, confirm to me that the situation is unstable and perilous, so freedom will wait.

— Good morning Sir. I'm Georges Writ, the director of this establishment. Glad you are there. The governor trusts you and extrols your praises to me. I hope you can solve this mystery before the situation gets out of control. The staff is very nervous with the presence of the animorphs outside. I'll take you to Miss Slat, the injured nurse.

We shake our heads, glancing around. I am convinced that the shapeshifters have spotted us. In any case, I felt them. Wolves.

— Can you tell me if anyone other than the nurse was injured?

— A doctor and one of his nursing colleagues were knocked out, but nothing comparable to what they did to Miss Slat. They violently attacked this poor woman. To believe that she was their main target. She would have died without the intervention of the guards. They were forced to fire on the attackers who then fled.

— Is one of the witnesses available to give us his version? Maybe a detail will help us understand what exactly happened.

— Of course. I'm sending you the nurse who was also there that day. She will join you in her colleague's room.

The nurse in front of me is in bad shape as far as I can see. Plaster on the arm and bandages that go down under the hospital gown, plus the wounds hidden by the sheet. They really tried to assassinate her. She looks so fragile, so sweet. Who would want to hurt such a pretty and tiny girl. She certainly did not provoke them. Something is missing. A young blonde woman, a bruise on her temple, enters the room and takes me out of my contemplation. I tend to be claustrophobic when there are too many people in a small room. So I signal to Owen and Liam to go out and keep an eye on the corridor. I will give them a summary later.

— Hello. I'm Ashley, a friend and colleague of Sevana.

— Connor. Can you tell me what happened to your friend?

— Not really. These two guys came in and knocked me out when I told them they couldn't stay there. I have been unconscious for a long time. I did not assist to the attack. All I can tell you for sure is that they originally came for the patient. They looked only at him when walking through the door.

That's more plausible than what happened later. It remains to be seen why events then went wrong and the answers are necessarily related to the woman lying on this bed.

— Okay. So tell me about your friend.

— Sevana is great and really brilliant at this job. Everyone appreciates her.

I feel uncomfortable. She twists her hands and avoids my gaze. I'm sure she's hiding something to me.

— Tell me everything you know if you really care about her.

— Are you really there to protect her? No matter who she is and what she can do?

Funny question. It looks like she's afraid that I will change my mind when I hear her answer.

— I work with the governor for this purpose. I will do everything in my power to ensure her survival. No one deserves to suffer like her.

The nurse looks at my eyes, as if to probe my soul, and resumes.

— She is unique. She is the best here. She always knows in advance when a patient is going bad.

The nurse then whispers a sentence to me that makes my heart jump.

— She has a talent.

We look at each other with Nate. I'm not sure I understand. It is impossible, but I am one of the optimists who hope that the fatels are hiding among us, that some of their children have survived. We are probably thinking of the same thing, because we are taking a deep breath at the same time. No, no olfactory trace of magic. Not surprising ,the fatels disappeared when I was just a kid. I only breathe the powerful smell of medecines that makes me sneeze. A final question will confirm that we were on the wrong way.

— Does Miss Slat have a physical particularity?

— A fault you mean? No, except that she is very pretty and yet single ...

I will have to be more specific.

— Um, nothing at her eyes?

— No, beautiful blue eyes, but that's all. You can see it for yourself in the evening. Coma is artificial. The experimental drugs of course work well on her, so we reduce them so that she woke up.

— Thanks for the information, Ashley.

She goes out after checking her friend's health.

— This story is weird, Connor. How can she have premonitions without being a prophetess? Magic that no longer exists, by the way.

— I don't know. We will have to wait until she wakes up to know.

Deafening noises in the corridor make us look up from Sevana.

— CONNOR, INTRUSION.

I half-open the door and note with fright that my friends are transformed and in the middle of a fight against wolves. Our arrival taught them that she was alive and above all, protected. They want to finish the job before she becomes unattainable. We have to get her out of there as soon as possible.

— Nate, the corridor is too narrow for your bear. You carry the nurse and you go behind. See you at the SUV. Be careful. She has to stay alive.

My buddy wastes no time. He takes off the infusion and the sensors, takes our protegee in his arms as comfortably as possible so as not to aggravate her injuries, and follows me to execute the plan. I get transformed and throw myself into a fight while Nate takes the opposite direction, taking advantage of the confusion to go unnoticed.

My cheetah wastes no time and directly bites a wolf on the neck, badly piercing the skin and causing blood to flow. The panther by my side opens its opponent's abdomen with its claws, spreading guts and intestines, while Liam's wolf pushes its opponent's head with sharp fangs as best he can. Owen took the opportunity to go behind and slaughtered the attacker of his buddy. The three wolves are dead and blood stains the floor of the corridor. We take on human form before the fearful gaze of the hospital staff who had stood aside from the danger and we end up in our simplest device. This is the drawback of untimely metamorphoses: our clothes cannot resist it. We borrow hospital pants and join Nate, who is wearing nothing but jeans, a dead wolf at his feet.

— A setback ?

— A clever boy was waiting by the car. Nice outfits. Green enhances your complexion.

— Stop joking. We have to go before other wolves fall on us.

I start driving, Nate at my side, while the infernal duo settles in the back, one on each side of the woman to support her, installing her as best as possible. She seems tiny between these two colossus, and more vulnerable. Liam brings me a truth that I already know.

— We can't go back to the territory. We don't know anything about this girl, she is too hurt to bear the trip and above all, I doubt that this clan of wolves will leave us alone. They want her dead and are ready to take risks to get there. Attacking a human hospital in broad daylight is a sign of great determination and a great deal of madness. So, an uncontrollable and dangerous pack.

I think exactly the same. That's why I'm driving at full speed, my eyes fixed on my rearview mirror to watch that we're not being followed, toward a land that the governor has specially made available to us an hour away. It was supposed to be our temporary refuge during the investigation, it will finally be our hideout.

As soon as we arrive, we install Sevana Slat on the bed, carefully covering her with the blanket and each one of us take turn in the shower to remove the stench of death that sticks to our skin and excites our animals. I need to update Sean on the latest events. He's our geek in the pack, I hope he can teach us something useful.

— I'm going to call Sean. We need information about this girl and the dead wolf who had been admitted to the hospital.

— With Liam, we're going to run.

— Okay, Owen. Nate?

— I stay here. Go and let off steam with them after your phone call.

— Thanks, I won't be long. See you soon.

Chapter 4

Connor

Running made me feel good, but the phone call from my beta immediately put my cheetah on edge. It didn't take him long to discover the clan responsible for this mess thanks to the corpses of wolves who attacked us at the hospital. The Black pack. I have an account to settle with them since two decades, even if I have no proof. Unfortunately, it is a powerful clan which it is better to avoid having contact with if we are attached to life. How did an orphan, adopted by a human family with no history, attract their attention?

I find Nate inside.

— You are anxious.

He knowns me well, and for a long time. He was one of the first shapeshifters I helped.

— A priori, it is a settlement of accounts within a clan. The victim wanted to change the pack. When his alpha found out, he ordered him to be beaten to death and to be thrown into an alleyway to serve as an example: this alpha accepts no departure. Things got complicated when humans found him and brought him to the hospital. Wolves are part of the Black.

— You always grumble as much when you mention them.

— No wonder. They are the murderers of my parents. I'm not going to forget it. It is better to change the subject.

— How's the girl?

— She's about to wake up.

— Okay. Go join Liam and Owen in the woods to get your bear out. I'm sure that it needs to go and rub the trees in the corner to mark it presence. I stay with her.

As soon as I got back into the chalet, my cheetah got on the alert and went around in circles. It is agitated and pushes me to go immediately to her bedside. My animal is however docile in normal times, few things disturb it. In addition, I hear the nurse breathing slowly and regularly, she is not yet awake, there is no hurry. It claps my jaw squarely, calling me an idiot. It’s the first time it wanted to take control without my consent. It is better to go see her or it will end up to claw me.The smell of medicines floats around her, less strong, but still present. However, another now surpasses it. Spring flowers and morning dew. Hell, that smell is bewitching. I lean towards Sevana to breathe it better and I perceive what my cheetah noticed before me thanks to its hunting smell: the bond of union. I just found my other half, my soul mate, my destiny. And she is hurt. Badly. My cheetah shows its fangs at this mention. The Blacks wanted to kill her. It is unacceptable. They will never take a loved one away from me again. I would not allow it. I am no longer a helpless child. I haven't told her yet that I'm already possessive and protective. Linked instincts are powerful.

I take this opportunity to observe her more carefully. She is very beautiful with a thin, pale face, high cheekbones and long black eyelashes above her almond eyes. I can't wait to see them open to dive into their ocean color that her friend Ashley described to me. Her black hair with blue reflections, like the wings of a crow, sprawls on the pillow like a halo over her head. She looks like an angel fallen from the sky. My angel to me. In addition, she is single. Her friend told me so. Fine, no competitor to eviscerate.

— What are you doing leaning over her?

I jump at Nate's voice. I turn around and see that my three friends are looking at me with question marks in their eyes. I was so absorbed in contemplating Sevana that I did not hear them coming.

— Are you purring?

Owen's hearing is formidable. I clear my throat. I owe them explanations. I don't want to pass for a pervert. And our plan of action will radically change too. It is out of question that my destiny will be in danger.

— Change of program. We drive her home, in the pack.

They look at me, dumbfounded. Liam, the most diplomatic, speaks for everyone.

— No witness on the territory. It’s your rule. Too dangerous for the pack. Especially since we don't know why they want her dead.

— Things are different this time.

— In what ? Do you have any new information?

— A crucial fact, yes. She is my soul mate.

It has the merit of silencing them. Nate takes over.

— Are you sure ? You haven't noticed it until now.

— How did you feel at the hospital?

— The smell super strong of meds and detergents.

I see that he understands when he speaks, because his eyes widen in surprise.

— It masked her own fragrance. Now that the treatment fades in her blood in the absence of an infusion and that it is no longer in a sanitized environment, you can see the connection.

— Exact. Even if the smell of the hospital is still present on her. But within a day or two, she won't have a trace of it.

Owen looks at me with envy. I understand that, it's our ultimate dream to find our other half.

— You're lucky, man. You found the woman of your life.

— I know. Only, she is in bad shape and I count on you to help me protect her until she is safe at home, at our home, in our territory.

They all respond in a beautiful set and I expected no less from them.

— We are ready to give our life for her. She is our alpha female.

For our people, females, especially soul mates, are sacred gifts that we must safeguard.

— Connor, I'm going to check her injuries, make sure they haven't gotten any worse during the drive.

Liam is our assigned therapist when needed. He studied medicine before joining us. He approaches, raises the plastered arm of my wife and lowers the blanket to the waist of Sevana. He then begins to open her hospital gown. My eyes are fixed on the hands of my friend who touches my angel.

— Connor, calm down. CONNOR.

Nate's shout brings me to my senses, my brain clouded with anger. I showed fangs to Liam and my eyes are those of cheetah. Shit. I blink several times to regain control. My pet gives way to me, but stays close.

— Sorry Liam.

— No problem. You haven't claimed her yours yet. Your cheetah will be on edge as long as the link is not final and will be possessive and jealous. But I really need to check that she's okay.

— I know. Just let me undress her myself and hide her chest. It will calm my beast a little.

They all close their eyes while I get active. I watch her as little as possible. After all, she is unconscious, this is not the time to rave about her body, but I still notice that she has pretty shapes, round and firm breasts in harmony with her flat stomach. My cock makes fun of the situation. It has been at attention since I smelled her, which doesn't help me stay detached.

— It's ok. You can heal her .

Liam gently raises the bandages on her belly and I start to growl in rage, but it's no longer against him. Besides, my companions growl as much as I do. My sweetheart has deep lacerations on her abdomen, claw holes on the flanks and many bites all along her clavicle. They immobilized her so they could inflict maximum damage on her. That does not make any sense. The Blacks didn't just try to kill her, they deliberately made her suffer. I can't hold back a roar of rage. This outburst of violence on my wife is unacceptable to me and my cheetah. Liam puts a hand on my shoulder in support. He too grits his teeth harder than necessary.

— Her wounds were significant, but they are half healed, she will get out. It's quick for a human.

— Her friend said they gave her experimental drugs.

Liam concentrates and frowns, which creates a wrinkle between his eyes.

— I think I know what treatment they gave her. Products probably created based on shapeshifters genes. I heard about it. Humans are testing them to speed the healing of serious and potentially fatal injuries. It will help her a lot and she should keep few scars.

This is good news, but even if it keeps traces of the attack, she will remain perfect and beautiful. Liam draws my attention to the next problem that we will face.

— However, she will soon wake up in an unknown place, surrounded by shapeshifters like those who attacked her, and she will be in pain. It's not ideal.

He is right. She will be scared, in panic, and therefore may worsen her injuries. She has many stitches, it is important that she stays calm so as not to tear the skin again.

— Wait outside. I stay with her. She should feel the bond between us, even if it is partial. It will soothe her and I will explain the situation to her.

— Okay. Shout when needed. She should not stir immediately or she will blow up her points.They all leave the room and I feel calmer with no other males around her. My cheetah curls up without taking its eyes off her and I bring a chair close to the bed and sit there taking her hand.

It's a groan of pain that wakes me up a few hours later.

Chapter 5

Sevana

The pain is unbearable. I try to turn sideways, hoping to find a more comfortable position, but a hand in mine prevents me. It's a large, solid hand holding mine with an iron handle without crushing it. I can't remember where I am, why I hurt so much everywhere, like a truck had rolled me over, and my eyes refuse to open.

— Hush, stay quiet. You are safe.

I frown. This voice is unknown to me, but I find it soothing, reassuring. I immobilize on my back and try to clear the fog from my mind. Why telling me I'm safe? Think about it girl. It's hard, my brain is clouded and my cogs are struggling to get going. I try to turn my head towards the presence that I perceive at my side, but bandages pull my skin from the neck. That's when flashes come back to me like so many dismal photos. Claws and fangs that pierce me, my blood flowing, a huge slimy puddle on the ground. I gesture, I want to run away from these monsters, but a hand begins to gently stroke my hair.

— Everything is OK, I promise you. You have nothing more to fear. You have to avoid moving. You're going to hurt yourself even more if you do.

It's decided, I like this deep and grave voice with a little smoothy side. I could listen to him for hours. I want to talk to him. My first attempt is difficult with my throat as dry as sandpaper.

— Waaaaaaatter.

— Wait a second.

He lets my hand and I immediately miss his warmth. I hear him move around the room. It’s confusing to be in total darkness.

— Here, drink softly.

One hand supports my head while another carries a glass to my lips. After a few sips, my throat loosens and the words are more fluid.

— Thank you.

— How do you feel ?

I hear that he places the glass on a piece of furniture by my side and he immediately takes my hand, drawing circles on the top with his thumb. It's pleasant and strangely relaxing. I do not forget the pain that twists my insides.

— I am in pain. Could you call a nurse?

He tightens his grip on my hand and I feel like hc's hesitating before answering me.

— We're not in the hospital anymore.

I tense up immediately. Where am I then? And why would the hospital have allowed me to go out when my condition is far from satisfactory in view of my suffering?

— Why ?

— You were in danger. With my team, we are responsible for protecting you.

I relax slightly. OK, there are people around to keep me alive, even if I don't know who and why I need it.

— Can you tell me what do you remember?

I collect snippets from my memory.

— I was helping to heal a shapeshifter , a seriously injured young wolf, when two men arrived and attacked everyone.

— Would you tell me about them?

No need to specify, I know exactly who he is talking about and my instinct tells me that I can trust him even if this certainty has no basis.

— They were shapeshifters. I could describe them for a robot portrait if you want.

— Later. Did you know them?

— No. I rarely see shapeshifters.

— Why this ?

I hear at his voice that he is intrigued. The stress unties my tongue, like every time.

— My parents always told me to be wary of them. That very few are trustworthy and that it was better for me to stay away from their people. They made me promise not to approach them except in the course of my work, only if they are about to succumb to their injuries.

He immediately stops the caresses on my hand and his grip becomes rigid without becoming painful or threatening. It's more like he's afraid I'm going to run away.

— So you hate us.

Shit. He's one of them and I just upset him. Please don't let him attack me too. It was not intentional and I never had a priori.

— No. I don't hate shapeshifters. Only I listen to my parents and my recent experience tells me that they were not wrong.

He relaxes slightly and returns to more on neutral ground.

— Why do these wolves mad at you?

— No idea. I had never met them before they rushed to the hospital to commit atrocities.

I’m trying to open my eyes, but it’s very painful. They are dry and my eyelids are glued. That's right, I was wearing my lenses when I passed out, so they must still be in place since no one knows I am wearing them. I will have to take them out if I want to distinguish something. They are not made to stay in place for ... how long actually?

— How many days have passed?

— Since your attack?

I nod imperceptibly.

— You were in a coma for a week.

— Wow. I'm in bad shape then.

— You're perfect and you're going to get over it.

OK. I am facing a smooth talker. A week without a shower, no comb, and no toothbrush, I'm certainly far from perfect. Not to mention my injuries, which must be significant given the dressings I can feel everywhere.

— I still need water, please.

I immerse my index finger in the glass he is holding out to me so that I can moisten my pupils and slide my lenses. I'm instantly less irritated, but I barely open my eyelids when I am dazzled by the bulb above my head.

— Ouch, the light.

He gets up and operates two switches. I then try again and flutters for a moment before directing my gaze to the man by my side, dimly lit by the diffuse light of the adjacent room.

— FUCKING SHIT.

His cry immediately makes me close my eyes without even having distinguished his silhouette and a lone tear runs down my cheek. I have not experienced this humiliating situation since I was a child when children made fun of me the only day I went out in secret. I had long thought that my parents were ashamed of me, of my oddity and that it was for this reason that they did not allow me to leave the house. That day, I realized that they mostly protected me from the wickedness of others. My parents later made me promise never to show myself without my lenses again and that on that condition, I could go outside as much as I wanted.

His cry also raked spectators. I see rushed movements. As if a disgusted look was not enough.

— Any problem Connor ?

— No no. I was just surprised.

I feel him approach me and wipes my tear from my thumb. I keep my eyes tightly closed.

— Forgive me. I did not expect that. I had no reason to shout. Open your eyes.

I shake my head in denial. Once will suffice me

ashamed.

— I can put on sunglasses if you have them. You will be more comfortable.

— Don't say stupidity. Your eyes are beautiful. I just was amazed at that moment.

I hesitate. I like his voice, I trust him without even knowing him and I'm afraid of being suddenly disappointed. I don't want to see his expression.

Their reactions to all. When I was a child, the children called me a monster. I am not sure that adults are more sympathetic towards my particularity. My parents thought the opposite anyway.

— Please.

He asks me with such kindness that I cannot resist. I slowly open my eyelids and his gaze dives into mine. He is so close that he hides me from newcomers and it’s better.

— You are unique. The miracle that many have hoped for twenty—five years.

He whispers that to me like it’s wonderful like if I don’t understand anything.

— I'm just screwed up. Nature's mistake. It's not a miracle, it's a curse.

Chapter 6

Connor

The way she talks about herself, I realize she has no idea what she is and the hope that she arouses in me. She thinks her eyes are defective while they are magic. I also better understand the recommendations of her parents. They made her suspicious of my people to protect her and I thank them for that. They intentionally kept her away from the animorphic world so that she would survive. They've hidden her from the world, mostly from the shapeshifters, for the past 25 years. I cannot believe that she really exists and that she is here with me.

— Trust me. Show your beautiful eyes to my friends.

She capitulates and accepts, not without reluctance. I push myself to the side, without moving away from her, and watch the amazement of my lieutenants appear on their faces.

— It's impossible. We would have felt it.

— Like how I should have felt the connection,

Nate?

— The drugs made us miss the essential. The Blacks discovered it by chance, coming to execute one of their own. That’s why they’re looking for her and they want to kill her. Someone did a bad job then and now they want to rectify that mistake. Why did her friend tell us she had blue eyes? She protects her?

— Colored contact lenses. They are in the glass. I don't think her friend Ashley knew about it, did she, Sevana?

She obviously answers me in the negative.

— No, no one has ever seen my eye color except my parents.

In reality, my wife has the most extraordinary eyes possible. A blue eye and a green eye. The magic minnows eyes of the prophetesses.

— She's probably the last of her kind. The Blacks will not leave her alive without fighting. They will hunt her down relentlessly so that she can never get in the way of their project. They still haven't given up on being the masters of the world.

— I know Owen. Do you still agree to help me?

They look at each other to decide.

— Of course. This girl is a miracle. And she is yours. The rest is insignificant.

I never doubted them. Like me, they deplore the inaction of our people in the face of the greatest massacre in history. We were only children, we did not understand the implications of the events. Today, everything is different, and we know that animorphs are not made to be leaders on earth. We act too instinctively, we are guided by our emotions and it is incompatible with impartiality.

A soft hand grabs my arm. Its heat goes back to my spine, my whole body vibrates under her touch. I help her straighten up and barely hold back from slipping beside her in the bed to take her in my arms.

— Can I know what you're talking about? Who is a miracle?

She is baffled and frowns, rolling up her pretty nose at the same time. She is adorable.

— Let me introduce you to everyone. My name is Connor and my lieutenants are from left to right Liam, Owen and Nate. We are part of the Guardian Angels pack and work closely with the governor as a close protection service.

My friends give her reassuring smiles and wave their heads or hands while she listens to me attentively.

— OK. And why do I need such great protection? I don’t even know why these animorphs attacked me and there’s little chance that it will happen again. I told you. I have no contact with your people.

— Let's start at the beginning. What do you know about your parents?

— They adopted me when I was a baby. They were friends with my biological parents who died in a car accident.

We look at each other and we nod. Yep, an accident surely orchestrated by the dissidents. There were many at that time. In reality, these biological parents are fatels, it is a certainty, had to voluntarily hide her with humans knowing that they were in danger. Other couples have had this idea, but I was convinced that none had succeeded. At least she knows she was adopted. It will always be one less psychological shock, because I will have to reveal the rest.

— Twenty-five years ago, right?

— Yes.

— Do you know what your parents were?

— I was barely a year old, I have no memory of them, but they were necessarily human since I am not shapeshifter.

She makes me smile. She is pragmatic, I will have to shake her up a bit in her beliefs.

— No, you're not a shapeshifter. However, you can

predict the future of your patients in the hospital, right?

She shrugs as if it's nothing special.

— Simple intuitions. Lots of people have it. It's nothing extraordinary.

— It's possible, but I'm sure you're the only one who can never go wrong. And you are also the only one with such special eyes.

I pause to give her time to assimilate all of these new data and then deliver the final blow.

— You have a talent Sevana . You are a prophetess.

She shakes her head from left to right, but interrupts, wincing, placing a hand on her bandages.

— Impossible. The prophetesses were fatels, weren't they?

I nod my head in agreement.

— All the fatels are dead. We were taught this in the course of history, even if we are not explained the circumstances of their disappearances or the reasons. So I can't be one.

— I really need to feel that.

Liam approaches without ceremony and sniffs her in the neck. Sevana has a sudden backward movement which pulls her a grimace and I, I roll up my lips. He may be my friend, he is too close to my female. Only me who have the right to drown my nose in her ink hair.

— Magic flows through her veins. The smell of meds had faded again. her essence resurfaces. Tomorrow, she will no longer be able to go unnoticed.

I groan at tearing my throat.

— Back off.

He raises his hands in the air as a sign of appeasement and moves back in reverse, staring at me, in case I jump on him.

— Connor, are scaring.

What does Owen say? Liam has never been afraid of me and his face expresses no fear.

— You scare your wife.

This stops my jealousy attack. I turn to Sevana and see her half curled up on herself, eyes closed and fists clenched, as if she was preparing for battle. Her whole body is trembling with dread. What an idiot ! I will slap myself.

— We'll leave you. We're going to prepare breakfast. She must regain strength and we too may need it.

— Thanks guys.

They all leave the room, leaving me alone with my

terrified soulmate.

I kneel near the bed to appear smaller and less scary and take her hand gently, loosening her point in stride. It is out of the question for my soul mate to fear me.

— Sevana, no one will hurt you here. I promise you. I would never get mad at you, and neither of my friends would. You are too precious for me and a miracle for others.

She tilted her head to the side and plunged her gaze into mine. I could get lost inside. I feel like she probes my soul.

— Do you really think I'm a fatel?

— Yes, a prophetess. I am sure.

— At the hospital, they said I shouldn't exist.

I clench my teeth and my fists and my cheetah tries to intervene, but I control my fury so as not to traumatize her any more.

— We will protect you and risk our lives.

— Why would you do that? Why am I so precious? Because I'm probably the last of my people?

— To begin. Yes, you may be the last fatel in existence, but you give me hope that others, like you, have managed to hide. Not all packs think like the Black pack chasing you, and what I said specifically is that you are precious to me.

— For you in particular?

She must feel the link between us, but I don't know if she knows the meaning, if she feels the depth.

— What do you know about soul mates among shapeshifters?

— shapeshifters have one true love that lasts a lifetime. They form a very united and inseparable couple together.

Okay, she knows the basics.

— Yes, and we recognize her instantly, it's visceral. It's like love at first sight, we feel an instant and unconditional love for the person who completes our soul like no other could. What many ignore, however, is that our soul mate is not necessarily animorph. You are mine Sevana.

She opens her mouth several times. She looks like a goldfish. It makes her a lot to digest in a short time. It's normal for her to be confused. I caress her cheek with the back of my hand. Her skin is soft like silk.

— We will have time to talk about this later. No rush. I have no intention to leave you. Do you want to get up to eat or do I give you the pecked in bed?

She laughs by shaking her head, but stops very quickly by touching her stomach.

— Stop the humor, it hurts. You would have

clothes for me. I'd love to be on my legs and the gowns are nice, but they let the air flows pass. A week in bed is enough.

— OK, no joke yet, it’s noted. Do you want to put on my t—shirt?

My pet needs you to smell it.

— It's weird, you know?

Necessarily. She just met me and I ask her to wear my clothes. It's not a trivial request, but my cheetah is possessive and pushes me to mark her. That should appease it while waiting for the link to materialize.

— Okay, if that keeps him from eating me raw.

— I thought we said no more jokes?

I like her character. Despite a perilous situation and a diminished physical state, she remains hopeful and does not lack humor. My cheetah yells at me that it is going to devour her and that she will love it.

She looks beautiful in my clothes. She is covered up to the knee, revealing the rest of her long shapely legs and I guess her generous chest without a bra. Damn, this is not the time to have an erection! I help her stand up. She arrives just at my shoulders and her soft, supple body molds perfectly to mine, like two pieces of a puzzle. I support her to go and sit at the table, her legs being stiff after several days of inactivity. I servc her a hearty plate and sit down next to her. Impossible to stay away from her, even a few steps. My pet is against it and I agree with him.

She will never be alone and defenseless again. She will always find a cheetah by her side in all circumstances.

Chapter 7

Sevana

I stare at Connor stealthily, finally lighted by daylight. He's a man with broad, muscular shoulders, with well-drawn biceps and abs, deep black eyes that match his short hair and the shadow of his beard on his square jaw. A real treat for the eyes. I have had boyfriends before, but they were still one hundred percent human and, objectively, much less impressive. Connor has this wild, animal side, which, instead of scaring me, attracts me irreparably towards him. By his side, my stress disappears. And he looks at me like a treasure fallen from the sky. I feel so desirable.

— Connor, you're drooling.

The man named Nate has a sense of humor too. Not bad in his genre either. He is larger and more square than my serving knight, but just as appetizing. I look at them with curiosity, the same way they do with me. I have before me four males as beautiful as gods, immense, and determined to keep me alive. What more? Satisfy my curiosity perhaps.

— Has any of you ever found his soul mate?

They suffocate on their sip of coffee. Nate even has liquid coming out of his nose. Only Connor hides his sneer behind his cup. I was just curious to know if there were other women in their pack. And secretly, I told myself that someone who had experienced the same upheaval as me would be able to explain to me the whirlwind of feelings that has exploded in my chest since I woke up. I have just been attacked, bleed to death by shapeshifters, and yet I have full confidence in Connor, and indirectly, in his friends.

— Did I say something stupid ?

He embraces my fingers and kisses my knuckles. We don't know each other, and yet that seems natural to me. I feel an indescribable link between us.

— You have the right to ask any questions you want, sweetie. And to answer this one, no, none of these lads is united. They have not yet find the woman created to support them.

Pity. So I would have to ask Connor for answers.

— Can I ask a question too?

I look at the young blond man on my left. He must be the youngest in the group, around my age. I have always had a good memory of their names and faces.

— Liam, right? I'm listening to you.

— How do you predict the future?

— I do not know. It's intuitive, natural. Sometimes I touch people and I know things.

— For example, just by flicking my hand, can you predict what will happen to me? Without even thinking about it?

— Not always, but yes, sometimes it happens to me. I don't really control it.

— Can we try ?

Connor brings me closer to him, preventing me from touching the hand that his friend holds out to me, and intervenes.

— Later. Sevana needs rest. Her talent could weaken her and she is already vulnerable.

He glares at his friend then turns to me.

— Besides, I'm sure you would enjoy washing yourself.

I scream, horrified.

— I stink, that's it! You have a lot of flair, sorry. I doubt the nurses at the hospital took the time to clean me.

I am embarrassed and probably scarlet. I would like

to hide in a mouse hole. Or at least have a bottle of perfume nearby.

He also makes fun of me! He laughs with outstretched throat, just like the other seated men!

— No, I love your smell. In fact, you smell the spring flowers and the morning dew. A true delight. I'm already addicted to it.

I didn't think I could be even more red! Even my skull heats me up to the roots of my hair. He knows how to compliment this guy. My heart melts a little more for him.

— Flattering. A shower would be great.

— Come on, I'll help you walk.

Connor leads me to the bathroom next to the bedroom I woke up in, hugging me.

— Thank you. I'll manage for the rest. You can go out.

— Don't wet your points or your plaster. You will not do it alone.

— Immediately remove this perverse smile from your face. You can't see me naked.

His mischievous smile and bright eyes are a constant temptation. And his little laugh burst bubbles in my stomach.

— You are my wife. I have the right to see

everything from you.

— I am ... I don't even know who I am anymore. Certainly not an easy girl anyway.

— We will make a compromise. You cover the most important parts of your anatomy with towels and you let me clean you.

It’s a good solution. In all honesty, I don't have the strength to do it alone, getting up got exhausted. So I accept his proposal, which gives him a satisfied expression.

— Sit down and let me do it.

This man could break me in two with a simple gesture and yet he acts with gentleness and tenderness. He conscientiously massages my scalp with the shampoo and then relaxes my painful muscles one by one, taking the time to untie each knot before soaping and rinsing me.

— You have magic hands.

His voice is even more hoarse when he speaks.

— I can show it to you differently if you want.

He does not lose time. I open one eye and realize that this cleanliness session had the opposite effect on him. He is tense… everywhere. A bump distorts his pants, making me warm.

— Maybe next time.

— Let me dry you and get you dressed.

Another oversized T-shirt and a man’s underpants rolled up at the waist. No matter, I'm clean and that's all that matters. I go back to sleep with a sigh of well—being.

— I need to kiss you. Just give me a kiss.

I immerse my eyes in hims and see only a pure and animal desire. He is so sure of himself. He sees my lack of protest as acceptance and melts into my mouth.

His lips touch mine, lightly, gently, igniting my senses and leaving me hungry. I am the one who prolongs the kiss, sliding my hand up his chest. He grabs me by the back of the neck, and leans my head back while our lips mix. His tongue slides gently over my mouth which opens to let it pass. I can hear myself groaning when his tongue dives inside, exploring it, tasting it. This man makes my head spin.

I step aside to catch my breath, and my mind at the same time.

— We must stop there.

— For the moment only. You are mine and so beautiful. It's hard to resist not to mark you.

— How does that marking me?

He sketched a backward movement and looked

away.

— Later. Liam has to do your bandages again.

Oh no, he's not going to run away. I already have a thousand questions on the tip of my tongue, out of the question that there is one more.

— I feel the bond between us, a multitude of feelings that I don't understand, which I don't know what to do, but if you want it to work between us, you have to be honest no matter what.

He sighs, hugs me and explains.

— To claim you, to permanently seal the bond of union that you feel, I must bite you.

I tense up and try to move away from him, without success, his arms are made of hardened steel around me. Only, concerning bite , I have already given.

— Is this what did the other shapeshifters do in the hospital? I belong to them?

— Don't be suspicious of me, please. And no, it is not the same thing. They sucked your blood to get stronger temporarily. This is one of the reasons for the extermination of the fatels. The blood of your people increases our strength tenfold when we absorb it, but the effects are time—limited. The claim mark is not painful, but aphrodisiac. It’s a mark of love.

I relax and watch his contracted face and tight lips.

I run my hand over his rough cheek.

— You are angry.

— They hurt you. It is unacceptable to me and my cheetah.

I would never have guessed the species of the animal that inhabits him. With his imposing size, I thought of a larger animal.

— Are you a cheetah? I would like to see it.

— It can't wait to rub you, but Liam has to take care of you first.

He goes to get his friend after a last kiss and a caress on my cheek. I can't wait to see this fierce animal who cares so much about me. I find it quite strange that Connor is sharing his body, thoughts and feelings with a wild animal.

— I'm going to disinfect your wounds and put a bandage on your stomach.

— Okay. Where's Connor?

— You must have noticed that he is very possessive. It is best to stay outside. He would be able to attack me for touching you, even if it's not sexual.

— I understand. Well I think. Go ahead Liam, I'm ready.

He acts with precise gestures, never touching my

skin directly. There is always a cotton ball or a strip of gauze between our epidermis. Until he fixed the last sticking plaster on my neck, touching my thumb lightly. This simple contact is enough for me to learn a crucial thing.

— Call Connor. Right now.

— Why ?

No time to procrastinate.

— CONNOR.

He rushes into the room, watchful.

— A problem sweetie?

— We have to leave. Right now.

Chapter 8

Connor

— Okay. EVERYBODY BY CAR. LET'S TAKE OFF NOW. You'll explain to me in the car.

I take her against me, one arm under her legs and one behind her, without wasting time. She puts her head on my shoulder and I could marvel at her if the situation was not so urgent. She must have had a vision, and that was not good news. She seems distraught.

Once the five of us are in the car, I start in high speed and we meet the threat she has perceived, a car full of snarling wolves, at the end of the road which leads to the chalet. I make a head to tail to avoid the head—to—head collision and run at full speed. Of course, our opponents turn around in a cloud of dust and then engage in a furious chase. My heart is beating a hundred hours as I stare at the rear view mirror and watch our pursuers far too close for me. Sevana's voice goes high, her anxiety is palpable.

— You have no weapons in this SUV?

I loosen my jaws to answer her.

— No sweetie. We are shapeshifters. We only fight with our claws and our fangs.

— In a car, your animals are useless without wanting to upset you.

She's right. My knuckles are white so I tighten the steering wheel so strong. The car behind us catches up and bumps into us at the bumper. The blow was not violent, but Sevana still groaned in pain. This situation is dangerous for her, even more than for us. The jolts may reopen her abdominal wounds which are only partially closed. My cheetah is mad with rage that we endanger the life of its companion and demands to be released.

— Connor, slowed down. I'm going to gain us time.

— I don't know what you think about Owen, but act quickly.

My friend comes off, opens his window and waits.

— My door at their hood.

— I do what I can.

I shift to the left and slow down slightly. Our pursuers take the opportunity as planned to go up on the right and give a steering wheel in our direction. At the time of the impact, Owen jumps onto their hood and breaks the driver's window in the same movement. I don’t take the time to watch the rest of it and step on the floor, finally putting some distance between the two vehicles.

As soon as they are out of sight, Nate asks me to leave him by the side of the road.

— Are you sure ?

— Wait for us a kilometer from here. Out of sight, but not too far. If I have to carry Owen, he makes his weight.

Always joking and fooling around. Like if it was th moment. But I trust him and follow his plan, even if I don't know what it is.

— How are you, sweetie, not too much sores?

She doesn't answer me and keeps her eyes closed. Too tense. I detach myself and turn around as best I can in my seat. I take her face in section. When she lifts her eyelids, her pupils shine, wet. She hurts and holds back her tears. I do not have time to comfort her that we hear far away a deafening noise of crumpled sheet metal and cattle roars. It didn't last more than five minutes, but the silence that follows ties my guts. I remain on the alert, in case it is necessary to leave quickly.

Finally, I see Nate and Owen, both standing, even if Nate is holding his ribs. I swap my place with Liam to take Sevana against me and we hit the road without delay.

What happened ?

— You know my bear, it wanted to play bowling. it ran into the car when it passed, and made it fly , making it roll over.

— My panther had the reflex to jump to the ground just before impact, as soon as it felt the presence of Nate, but not before having slit the driver's throat. He smelled of wolf and magic. How is it possible ?

My cheetah growls and rolls up my lips when I explain to them.

— Two Black men drank Sevana's blood at the hospital.

— They are powerful and can track her thanks to her blood. She is like a headlight in the night for these two sadists.

Liam groaned at his remark. He saw the bites and enraged as much as I did.

— There was only one with that smell in the car.

— Are you sure, Owen? The smell of spilled blood could mask the presence of the second.

— No, only one. I'm not making a mistake.

I hug my soul mate a little more and think aloud. The threat has therefore not been entirely eliminated.

— The assault dates back eight days. The last wolf will be able to track Sevana for about ten days before the blood ingested has no effect. So we have to hide her for two more days. Afterwards, they will be unable to find her. Particularly on our territory. In the meantime, we must direct them away from ours. Honey, we're going to be brave, we're going to have to travel a little more.

I look at her, but she doesn't react. Her head is on my chest, her hair hides her face from me.

— Sweetie ? SEVANA!

I raise her head with a finger under her chin and I feel like she is just a rag doll between my arms. In the midst of a panic crisis, I hadn't even noticed that Liam had parked and that Owen had gone out to let him his place. My friend carefully lays her down in the back seat and this position reveals a bloodstain on her T—shirt. Lost in anxiety, I am unable to remain rational. My body is contorted between my two forms. I am fighting metamorphosis.

— Connor, Connor. Listen carefully. Her heart is beating and she is breathing.

My cheetah takes over and confirms me saying Liam. I breathe deeply several times, and regain my calm.

— What does she have ?

— She's passed out. It's a pain reflex. Look, some stitches have skipped.

— The stress of the chase had to make her contract the abdominals beyond what was possible with her wounds. We're going to take shelter and I'll fix it.

— OK, here we go.

Owen takes the wheel after a call to Sean to explain the situation to him. He found us an isolated hideout six hours' drive from our position. I don't like the idea of Sevana suffering for so long, but I agree with my lieutenants. The wolves killed earlier must have had reinforcements waiting. It is better to move away as quickly and as far as possible.

— Hold on sweetie. I promise you everything will be fine. I will take care of you.

I clench my teeth and hold her against me, plunging my nose into her hair to control myself.

Chapter 9

Sevana

I wake up again in an unknown bed. It shouldn't become a habit. I try to move, but unlike the last time, it is not possible, but a whole hot body prevents me. A warm body, shirtless and muscular that I caress on the ribs.

— You tickle me sweetie.

I look up and find myself trapped in two black irises filled with gold glitter. Then these pupils lengthen, taking the shape of those of felines, before returning to normal.

— What was that ?

— My cheetah wanted to make sure that you were fine.

— It's the case. Even if I have no idea how I ended up in this bed.

— You passed out in the car. Liam must have made you some points again. The good news is that we should be quiet for a few hours while the wolves recover their dead. Can you explain to me what you saw? You knew we had to run away right at the right time.

I never talk about my visions. It's strange to be able to discuss it with someone.

— I saw Liam seriously injured. In fact, he was more like a wolf, with a deep gash on his stomach, but since he was the only one who touched me, I guessed his animal was a wolf.

— A wolf that touched you.

He scolds his thinking more than he talks. He is jealous !!! Liam wasn't kidding about Connor's possessive addiction.

— Stop snarling. He touched me while treating me, nothing more.

I put myself a little more against him to reassure him and because I have to admit that feeling his warmth against me is soothing. I barely know him, but I am irreparably attracted to him.

— You are mine, no one has the right to touch you.

— Don't say stupid things. My talent would no longer be useful in this case. I have to touch a minimum people to be able to help them.

— You're mine.

OK, jealous and stubborn. But also really really sexy.

— Don't look at me like that, it makes me want to eat you.

I blink several times.

— I look at you normally.

— No sweetie. You have a spark of desire in your eyes. It excites me.

He strokes my back with his fingertips, from the nape of the neck to the bottom of the kidneys, leaving a trail of chills in his wake. I can't resist and kiss him from the tip of the lips. The innocent kiss I instigate quickly turns into something more carnal. Our tongues glide over each other in a sensual dance, flying a cloud of butterflies in my belly. Connor ends it a little abruptly.

— We have to stop where I can't control myself and jump on you.

He sticks his pelvis to me and I feel his erection.

— You must rest. Let your body heal.

I am frustrated, but he is right. I am not in condition to do crazy things on my body and have known him for so short a time. However, I would lick the golden and silky skin well under my hand.

— All that I feel, the feelings which turn in my head and my heart, you feel them too?

— Yes. Tenfold, because my cheetah feels them too, but in a more primitive way. The magic of the bond is very powerful. It amplifies the feelings that would have taken time to develop between two creatures, like a love at first sight.

— Show it to me. I want to see how your cheetah is.

— Are you sure ? I don't want to scare you.

— I'm its female, it won't hurt me.

He smiles at me and stands up, satisfied of my answer. I am sure of myself. Connor wouldn't hurt me and I'm sure his animal is just like him.

He takes off the only piece of clothing he was wearing: underpants. I'm suddenly hot my cheeks are probably scarlet. His buttocks are a work of art, firm and full of muscle, and the rest, let's say, is a call to sin. I really want to stay quiet, but don't overdo it. Not very Catholic images are spinning in my head at the sight of this body that makes my mouth water. His smile widens and his eyes are teasing.

— You want me to stay a moment like that, maybe?

I run my tongue over my suddenly very dry lips, which gives him a groan. I am not the only one who is frustrated.

— You better hide all that under a fur.

He laughs and his transformation begins. his bones crack, move, his size becomes thinner and hairs cover it. The process takes no more than a minute and a beautiful cheetah is now in front of me. It must be within a meter high by a meter fifty from the snout to the tip of its tail. It has yellow fur speckled with black circle and its eyes are pure gold. I am captivated, it is magnificent. It approaches me like a predator, without letting go its eyes from me, and yet I have no fear. On the contrary, the same feeling of security that I feel near Connor lives in me. Once climbed on the bed,it rubs its muzzle against my neck and breathes my hair. I take this opportunity to stroke it between the ears. It is so soft, like a stuffed animal, and it purrs in my ear. I lie down and pat the mattress so that it settles down next to me. I feel its warmth through the sheet. It's so nice that I go back to sleep and stroke its spine, lulled by its purring.

We are both awakened suddenly by a very tall blond stranger, who enters the room knocking the door against the wall. My cheetah, still against me, growls, but does not make any attack, and the man, who remains by the door, does not seem dangerous or surprised by the presence of a wild animal in the room. He smiles at us with all his teeth while staying away from the bed. Wise precaution.

— Hello. I'm Sean. I wanted to talk to Connor, but he's a little too hairy to make conversation.

I smile. My stuffed animal is licking my chin and rubbing its nose behind my ear.

— You're drooling my dear, that's enough.

— It imbues you with its smell. It’s a shapeshifter reflex.

I turn to the newcomer.

— I'm already carrying its stuff, isn't that enough?

— It didn't mark you, so wants its smell to be everywhere on you while waiting. So that each male recognizes its smell on you and knows that you are not free.

As if to confirm, the cheetah rubs its head on my valid arm.

— Enough Connor. You're not going to pee on me to mark your territory!

It looks like he's sneering, it's a slightly disturbing throat noise. As for Sean, he bursts out laughing frankly.

— Don't give it that kind of idea, it will be able to. Come on pal, let's talk. I'm waiting for you in the kitchen.

He comes out as he entered and I really make a disgusted grimace.

— Don't even think about it, big boy. I am not a tree.

Chapter 10

Connor

Sleeping with my partner was blessing for my cheetah. It never felt so peaceful. It lies in a ball inside of me while I take human form next to Sevana, who is watching me with curiosity.

— Is the metamorphosis painful?

I take her hand and kiss her knuckles. I believe it will be a ritual for me. This allows me to touch her soft skin and taste her flavor at the same time.

— No. It's a natural process for me, like breathing. Or for you to predict future events.

— Alright I understand. And who is Sean? Your cheetah was not wary. And much less jealous than you.

— Sean is the beta of my pack and my friend. And my cheetah would have scratched until blood if he had tried to approach you. I would love to know what he's doing there. He was supposed to stay on our territory.

I sit up to get out of bed, but I stop before I'm out of

reach.

She caresses my back and the blanks and her hand leaves a trail of fire in her wake. Each touch inflames my senses. My excitement, which had subsided during our nap, resurfaces even more.

— We have to go see Sean my beautiful. Stop touching me or we won't get out of this bed for hours.

— Um, yes. But you should get dressed first.

Her eyes sparkle with envy and her gaze roams my body. She doesn't seem convinced by what she tells me. On the contrary, I think she prefers me naked. My body reacts in a quarter of a second under her glowing glance. I throw myself on her mouth, wrapping my arms around her, grabbing her buttock in passing. Unfortunately, the animorphs in the next room remind me of their presence.

— We can hear your groans.

— And we can feel your excitement.

My soul mate hides her head in my shoulder.

— Tell me they're kidding.

— Sorry sweetie. Owen has excellent hearing and Liam has exceptional smell. We cannot hide anything from a band of shapeshifters who are too curious for their own good.

These idiots sneer.

— Always threats in the air, Connor. You will never do anything to us. You can't do without us.

I give her one last kiss and finally get up reluctantly. No chance that these fools leave us in peace.

— We'll continue later. We will soon be quiet at home. No neighbor nearby to disturb us.

She gives me a resplendent smile that makes my heart jump in my chest.

We go into the kitchen hand in hand and I sit around the table with my friends, Sevana on my lap.

— So Sean, what are you doing here? Is the pack safe?

— I delegated it to three trusted leaders. Don't worry. You know that our territory is impregnable.

He is right. The advantage of this former military base which serves as our territory is that it is isolated and surrounded by multiple fortified enclosures. Walls, barbed wire, electric wires. So many obstacles, associated with invisible traps, which make our territory inaccessible to those who are not welcome there.

— I also told myself that you would need reinforcements and I wanted to see your partner.

The first reason is legitimate and welcome, in view

of the latest events, but the second makes me show the fangs.

— She's mine. You don't approach her.

Sevana wraps her arms around my neck and plays with the hair on my neck.

— I don't move my teddy bear. Don't be angry. You see that you are more jealous than your feline.

I stare at her, stunned, while the others giggle.

— I'm not a stuffed animal !

— Of course not. You are my big bad cheetah.

These fools laugh more and more. I chew on my partner's ear lobe as punishment and resume the conversation.

— Why did you want to see her?

— I want her to tell me about her talent.

My wife tilts her head to the side and continues.

— I already said what I knew. I was born with it and it manifests itself through touch.

— This is where you are wrong. Prophetesses don't need physical contact to have visions. Only the young fatels needed it. As adults, it was enough for them to focus on someone, even a distant one, to be able to predict the future. It is thanks to this ability that they were able to live in recluses. It allowed them to help people without being in their presence.

— How do you know ?

I doubt he will answer this legitimate question after all. Sean never dwells on his past, even with our pack companions.

— No matter. But you have to practice from a distance to develop your magic. Fatels children trained with adults to develop their talent. You were not so lucky and your power remained in the larval stage. You just have to work it to acquire more power.

She looks at me and I know she doubts.

— You will get it sweetie. I believe in you.

She nods and closes her eyes as I place her on a chair so that she doesn't physically touch anyone. I feel her concentrated at first, then very quickly frustrated, to end up really exhausted after half an hour.

— It's impossible. I can't do it.

Sean is looking at me. I know this expression. He will make a decision that will not necessarily please me. However, taking risks has saved us more than once.

— Sevana, I'm going for a ride with Liam, Nate and Owen. When we come back, one of us will attack Connor for the only purpose of hurting him. If you don't want him to be hurt, tell him who to watch out for and where the danger will come from. I warn you, we will not hold our blows.

She immediately panics.

— No, don't do that. I really tried. I can't do it.

They go out without listening to her beg. I know they won't hurt me badly, Sean just wants to motivate my other half. But she does not know it and is panicking.

— Give me your hand. Please.

— Calm down. Take a deep breath and think of me, of us. You are strong. I know you can do it. Help me stay as beautiful as I am now.

She gives me a weak smile before closing her beautiful minnows eyes and I feel our bond of union tense. She uses it to touch my mind with the thought this clever little one. She opens her eyes suddenly.

— Nate, by the window.

I barely have time to shift that my friend emerges out of the window and falls head—first onto the table. My dodging at the last moment knocked him over. Perfect. It will be my revenge for the bump the other day.

— Well done sweetie. You deserved a hug.

We pass in front of my lieutenant who rubs the egg appearing on his forehead and the other members of my pack who look at my fatel with admiration. My soul mate learns quickly, in addition to being beautiful and having humor. With a little training, her power will be limitless.

Chapter 11

Sevana

I never thought my talent could be improved. I had never been encouraged to use it either. My parents were the kind of people who said to me, "Don't get noticed, don't use this ability". Connor leads me outside. A forest borders the small house we occupy. It's great to breathe outside. I feel like it has been an eternity since I have taken some fresh air. He embraces me and we walk side by side while staying within sight of the house. Our four roommates do not lose sight of us. I feel like a curious beast. The main attraction at the zoo. Connor notices my glances towards the quartet.

— We are too far away for them to hear us. On the other hand, they will notice immediately if you put your hand on my buttocks.

— I'll just touch in front then.

He looks at me and we laugh together. Things seem so simple at his side that we could almost forget that we are on the run, and for my part, threatened with death.

— Tell me how you created the Guardian Angels pack.

Connor's face immediately darkens and he hugs me a little tighter. I will almost regret this question. But I need to know who he is before I commit to him. I understand that among the shapeshifters, the bond of union is final.

— As a kid, I lived in a pack of cheetahs, the Fauve pack. Our alpha was a good and just man, always ready to help his neighbor, and who believed in the merits of the hierarchy established between humans, fatels and shapeshifters. I was raised on the principle that everyone has a place and importance in the world. When the fatels began to disappear, he wanted to investigate, then intervene, learning about the involvement of certain animorphs packs, without going to war with ours. He went to see the fatels with his lieutenants to help them defend themselves. Unfortunately, when they arrived, the fatels neighbors of our pack had already been massacred. Most of the fatels were dead and the rest were on the verge of death from their injuries. A telepath, before his last breath, communicated to them the location of a cave where they had hidden their children. Couples, including my parents, volunteered to take in these orphaned and traumatized miracles. My family, like the others, was decimated two days later. I was eight years old. It was the Black people the responsables

They murdered all the families who had housed fatel people, as well as these children with extraordinary talents. Only young cheetahs were spared. We were to serve as an example. Real proof that the Blacks are not monsters because they could have crushed us, but because they had shown leniency.

I wrap my arms around his waist and place my cheek on his chest. The slow rhythm of his heart soothes my pain for him, for his broken childhood. I didn't know my biological parents, but those who adopted me loved me like their own daughter and, I realize today, they have protected me during their lives. I understand his resentment towards this rebellious pack. It already took everything from him.

— What happened next ?

— The alpha took in the orphans, but refused to explain the events to the higher instances of the animorphs. He was afraid to testify and I blamed him. At that time, I vowed to do everything to ensure that injustices will be punished in the future. So that such an injustice never happens again. As an adult, I learned that the governor wanted to set up a protection unit specializing in these delicate situations. Humans were aware that they were powerless against the actions of certain packs. I volunteered, as did Sean. We started two. Then some rescued animorphs wanted to stay with us.

This is how the pack was formed. It is called the Guardian Angels because our members say that is what we stand for them: Guardian Angels. They elected me alpha and Sean became my beta.

— Which explains why you all have different animals.

— Exact. Our pack is unique.

— You are a good person, Connor.

I kiss him and he lifts me up to deepen our kiss when we are interrupted by hissing.

— Real kids, your pack mates.

— Our pack bond is strong. It comes from a conscious choice and not from our birth or our species. And they like you. We are their alpha couple.

— Yep. They respect us, but not enough to leave us a little privacy, a priori.

He laughs and hugs me a little more against him. Our bubble of well—being bursts suddenly when I push him hard on the side, unfortunately too late: a dart is stuck in his arm. He yells to break his vocal cords: "LIGHTING", while forcing me to squat and leaning on me, making his body a human shield.

— Connor? It's okay ?

— I'm fine sweetie. Tell me you have nothing.

— It wasn't me who was targeted. I'm sorry, I should have expected. I am so sorry.

Tears start to run down my cheeks without that i can control myself. I am very attached to him, I should have protected him as he does for me. I was so taken up with our conversation that I only had my vision at the last moment, too late to foil fate.

Connor gently wipes my face, his eyes filled with love for me.

— Calm down sweetie. I feel good. It's nothing.

Liam comes running towards us.

— Are you both okay?

— Yeah. Sean caught the intruder?

— Yes, but we won't get any information. He struggled and the lion disemboweled it .

The wolf pulls the dart out of the alpha's arm and sniffs the tip.

— I do not recognize the product. Do you feel something strange?

— No. Nothing special. Let's go into the chalet.

Connor walks at my side with a stiff step. I take this opportunity to hold his hand and try to see his future, but do not feel anything specific and Sean's vision covered with blood, does not help me to ignore what is happening around. I breathe in several times through my nose and breathe out through my mouth to slow down the beating of my heart and focus again on Connor, on our partial union that I recognized earlier. And what I find fills me with dread. The dart was not aimed at Connor, but at his cheetah. My legs wobble and Connor catches me just before I collapse on the ground. I can't help sobbing while talking to him.

— Your cheetah ...

— He sleeps, surrounded by your smell. He is perfectly fine.

— No, it doesn't sleep.

He frowns and sweat begins to run down his temples.

— He doesn't wake up. I can't transform myself.

— Your animal is in a coma. It disturbs my panther and I guess it's the same with your animals.

All the men agree with Owen's words and their faces reflect growing concern. The beta then summarizes the situation.

— They drugged our alpha animal to weaken it and weaken our pack at the same time. They will wait a few hours to be sure that the product has worked and to attack us in force. We won't have a chance to get out of it Liam, can you cure him?

— No. I don't know the composition of what they

used so it's impossible to make an antidote and even if it's the opposite, it would take too long. But there is a solution. Sevana could probably cure him.

I find hope in these words and it was about time, because I was really starting to tell myself that we were all going to die through my fault. I guess this is the same product injected into my canine patient in the hospital. I then understand how it works. It prevented him from healing by blocking his animal part. Without the animal, only the human part remains, much more vulnerable.

— How can I help him? I would do anything for him.

— You must seal your union immediately.

I tense up instantly. I know what it means. A new bite. More fangs planted in my flesh. Even though Connor told me it had nothing to do with what I went through in the hospital, feeling teeth on me again is not good for me.

— Your blood would give him the strength to wake up his cheetah.

I see what he means. Connor explained to me the power of fatel blood on the body of shapeshifters, but I don't know if I am mentally capable of enduring another injury. On the other hand, I feel a strong bond for my cheetah and I don't want to lose it. I hesitate then that Connor is more categorical.

Chapter 12

Connor

— No. I will claim her when she's ready and she wants it for the right reasons, not before. Find something else.

— Connor ...

— I said no Liam. End of the discussion.

All of them shake their heads in a sorry tone, except my soul mate, who looks to my eyes and shakes my hand.

— Leave us boys. I need to talk to Connor face to face.

— We'll be outside. We are going to monitor the perimeter to make sure there are no other immediate dangers.

My wife seems on the verge of fainting. She is white as a cloth and trembles with all her limbs.

— Don't worry sweetie. I won't mark you.

— Connor, would that save you?

— This is not a valid reason to do it.

She drops on the sofa, more exhausted than ever. More weary too. The latest events have taken her courage and determination.

— You didn't answer my question. Would it free your cheetah?

I don't want to force her , but I promised myself not to lie to her. Our relationship must have a solid foundation, it necessarily involves honesty and trust.

— The fatel blood makes us stronger, so yes, it would probably counter the poison. But I will never ask you that. I told you, it's an act of love. It shouldn't become a matter of survival. You deserve better.

I sit next to her and take her in my arms. Her smell is intoxicating, I would cover her with kisses to reassure her and make her forget everything. That she has only us in mind. Our paths crossed in the worst possible circumstances.

— What are you feeling for me?

I have no hesitation.

— You are my Everything. You are my soul mate.

— This is not what I mean by that. This is only the bond of union. But how do you feel?

— You are beautiful, intelligent and courageous. I liked you as soon as I saw you on your hospital bed, even if it was not the ideal place to find yourself pretty. I love you more than anything.

She moves and settles in my lap, arms around my

neck, nestling her face in the crook of my shoulder.

— Mark me.

My cock stands up to the idea of taking her while I bite her and I curb my urges.

— No sweetie. Not like this. And not here.

— You told me it was an act of love. But you love me and I fell in love at first sight when you looked at my eyes in amazement. You are the first person who did not look disgusted with this vision. You accepted me as I am, as a whole. I told myself a long time ago that the day I meet the man of my life, he would stay with me until the end. I want to do it to help my stuffed animal, but especially because I believe in us.

I smile with all my teeth. A stuffed animal, huh? Unfortunately, I cannot mark her during a sexual act even if I am dying to do and as it is usually done. Her stomach wounds are still too fragile. But I can still make it very pleasant for her. And real torture for me.

— Sit astride me sweetie.

She complies without difficulty and without fear, and raises an eyebrow when feeling my erection against her intimacy, only separated by my jeans and underpants. The temptation is intense.

I kiss her tenderly, taking the time to explore every corner of her mouth, while gently removing the bandages on her collarbone. I trace with my fingertips the fine scars that remain. Gene therapy has really worked wonders. I will bet that her arm is consolidated.

I stick her to my chest and feel her chest pressed against me. I grab her buttocks and suck her moan in my mouth. I mix my tongue with hers in an erotic ballet and begin a back and forth movement with my cock against her clitoris. I collect each sigh and scream with my mouth, never stopping and the pressure builds up in her body. Her hands grasp my hair and a final rub against her crotch is enough to make her utter a cry of ecstasy. I choose this moment to place my mouth in the hollow at the base of her neck, planting my teeth deeply in it. I then feel my partner's muscles contract in successive waves, prolonging her orgasm, while I revel in the rich flavor of her blood. I finish my mark by licking her skin so that it closes while leaving an unequivocal scar. Once my darling has come down from her cloud, I make sure of her state of mind. I hope she has no regrets, because going back is impossible.

— How do you feel ?

She looks up and her languid look makes my penis jump, still as compressed behind my zipper.

—You can't imagine how me too, but I'm afraid we don't have time. We'll catch up soon, I promise you.

She then gives me a fiery kiss full of promise and we regretfully leave the comfort of the sofa to establish a plan with my friends. Our future depends on it. It is time to permanently eliminate the threat that hangs over her so that we can return home and have a peaceful couple life. We are assaulted by the group as soon as we pass the door.

— Congratulations alpha. It worked? Has your cheetah emerged?

— It exults and is very impatient to be alone with its female. Any plan, Sean?

Chapter 13

Sevana

It worked. My companion’s pet is back with us again. I can even hear it purring in my head. It’s a strange and reassuring feeling. I also feel all the love and passion Connor has for me. I land again on earth at the insistent voice of the beta.

— Sevana, are you with us?

— Sorry, I'm listening to you.

— You'll have to help us. I need you to focus on the wolf that attacked you so that we learn as much as possible.

— Okay. There were two of them in the hospital. Which one died?

— Owen?

The lieutenant thought for a moment before answering.

— Short black hair, dark skin, a little smaller than me. Nate?

— I didn't notice anything more.

I take the time to dive back into the most painful memories of my life. what about the bigger. The one with a scar on the cheek that seemed to give the orders. Connor intertwines our fingers and places a kiss on my forehead as a sign of support.

— Its good. I know which one is alive. The second had long, black hair and a gash on his face. Give me two minutes, I need to focus.

— Sit on me sweetie. Fix your back against me. I'll massage your shoulders, it'll help you relax.

Relax, I don't know, but get excited, surely. I close my eyes and see the enemy wolf. I haven't forgotten his face or that dismal shadow in his eyes. It’s surprisingly easy unlike the last time. Almost too much. What I perceive makes me screem in terror. Connor then whispers in the hollow of my ear.

— Come back to me sweetie. Look at me. What you see is just a possibility for the future. Help us change the future.

I can't stop stammering.

— Okay. They, uh, they'll be there in, uh, in two hours.

— Take your breath sweetie. I'm here, with you, we will protect you all.

— And who will protect you?

Nate touches me on the shoulder with compassion

and Connor's groan gives me a weak smile.

— We will protect our alpha as we will protect you. You are our alpha couple and as such, we owe you loyalty at all costs.

These men are adorable. They are fierce and hardened fighters, but I'm still afraid for them. My vision is far from encouraging.

— It is out of question that someone will die there.

— So tell us everything you saw.

— They attack us in the house and Nate has no place to get transformed.

— Humpf, my bear is a big oaf, it never passes in the corridors.

His remark has the merit of relaxing the atmosphere.

— You are badly injured right away and Owen, soon after, wanting to help you. He is attacked by two wolves simultaneously. Sean, Connor and Liam, you fight on your own, but you hinder each other and ...

— It's good sweetie, we got the idea. So there will be five wolves?

No, the chances would have been fair in this case and the Blacks are certainly not fighting fairly.

— Rather eight. I saw three of them out the

window, in addition to the five inside.

— Okay. The best way to avoid this catastrophic scenario is for the clash to take place outside.

— Perfect. That way I could release my bear.

Sean nods and continues.

— Owen should stand at the top of a tree, as a reinforcement, so that he can jump on the enemy's back and kill him quickly. Sevana will stay indoors, safe from the fighting. She shouldn't be hurt again.

I don't want to let them fight alone for me, but I know I won't be of any use to them. Connor would probably even put himself in danger to save me and that is unacceptable to me. I have a heavy heart and morale in my socks.

— I feel your anguish my beautiful. Let's all eat, we have to gain strength.

— I feel the joy of your cheetah. Is it happy to fight?

— No. It is overjoyed that you are ours. As much as me. Despite the situation, we are it and I delighted to have you as a companion and that our bond is final. Come on, I'll feed you.

Nate passes the meal joking. He's the comedian of the band. Sean does not loosen his jaws. Owen and Liam squabble over the style of their next conquest. A priori, they like to share. Yuck. Connor does not take his eyes off me and caress either my back or my thigh. I suspect him of continuing to mark me with his smell, but I'm certainly not going to complain. All the attention he has for me brings tears to my eyes. I have a companion and he is wonderful. I just joined a united family with very different members, but all endearing in their own way. I pray not to lose them in the hours that follow.

Unfortunately, time flies at full speed and soon they have to reach their defense position. I stop Liam, just before he follows Connor.

— Can you take my plaster off?

— Now is not the time. Why now ?

— An intuition. I feel it is important.

— Okay. Your bone must be reweld anyway. Do not move.

He leaves impressive claws and cuts the resin above and below over the entire length.

— It's OK. I have to join the others. Pay attention to yourself. Don't move from here.

Chapter 14

Connor

Even if i feel euphoria due to the pack union, my joy is tarnished by the anguish of my partner. The worst part is that she is not afraid for her life, but for mine and that of my friends. She's in love with me, even though she hasn't admitted it yet, and is afraid of losing me. No way. I just found her and I hope to have a future with her. A happy future, with mini cheetahs, who knows.

I stand near the trees, near the one on which Owen is perched, and free my feline. The wait is short. Sevana's estimated time of arrival was fair, not that I doubted her. We hear a few twigs cracking far away. Eight wolves arriving together, that necessarily makes a minimum of noise, even when they try to be discreet. My animal is on the lookout, ready to defend its female until death if necessary, and as if boosted with anabolics thanks to the fatel blood of my beloved.

The first wolf, of impressive size, entirely black and a scar from the muzzle to the right ear, the Head of this detachment for sure, comes out at the head of the undergrowth, lips rolled up on nasty long fangs. Followed by the others, in close formation. They all turn their heads in our direction, having spotted our smell. The fight begins when one of them leaves the group, probably attracted by the scent of Sevana, to head towards the house. No matter how safe she is in the building, the huge red wolf will have no problem entering it with its claws. And in front of it, my love will be defenseless. It’s Sean who blocks its path by landing in front of its muzzle, slaughtering its large lion paw on this one.

As the leader approaches me, I see that he is not an alpha. As usual, the pack leader remained in the shadows. This is how the rebel packs were able to act with impunity. If rebels were caught, the alpha claimed he knew nothing, that members of his pack had deserted and acted without his consent. The alpha then inflicted serious punishment on the members who had been caught, not for their abominable acts, but for having drawn attention to them. However, I'm sure it was the wolf who attacked my angel. She mentioned a scar on his face and that’s the only thing we keep from our transformations. I'm going to make it pay for the harm it did to my partner.

Assailed by my dark thoughts, I do not see until the last moment the black wolf which leaps towards me all claws outside. Fortunately, my buddy ensures my rear and the wolf is catapulted further by a huge grizzly bear which has tumbled on the left like a cannonball. When I turn my head to find my attacker, I see that Liam and Owen are not to be outdonc, surrounded by three fierce—looking lupine forms. The trio are used to interacting together. They each jump in turn without ever being shy, distributing a blow of claws that cut into the flesh and a blow of fangs that weaken.

My lieutenants are tough, but I can see that they struggle to repel them and take bad shots even if they give a few. Nate, closer to them than me, tries to join them to help them, but he is stopped by two gray wolves who jump on his back shamelessly, right between the shoulder blades, a place inaccessible to the paws of the bear. Nate bangs his back several times against a tree to dislodge them, but his opponents still had time to inflict ugly injuries before falling to the ground.

The leader then jumped on me by surprise, helped by one of his fellows. The two of them are much heavier than me. My cheetah rears up and swings its legs in all directions to claw them and regain freedom of movement. I manage somehow to slash the blank of the smallest, but the black takes advantage of it to plunge its fangs deep into my hind leg, destroying any possibility of escape. I just lost my best asset: speed. Anyway, I would never have left without my soul mate. To make matters worse, I feel by our bond that Sevana has perceived my pain and is literally terrified.

I watch my guardian angels out the window and see in horror that things look bad. Very bad even. Sean is about to bring down a red wolf, but he's the only one who seems to come out victorious from his duel. Nate is holding two wolves at bay, but remains trapped near a tree and the fur of his bear drips, creating a pool of blood on the ground, Owen and Liam are cut to pieces by three wolves despite reprisals well felt, as for Connor, he seems in as bad shape as his friends and limps around, his pain and concern for me reaching me through our link. I am terrified, but also angry.

I am in a terrible anger which boils my blood in my veins. I feel an intense power circulating in my body, so immense that I find it difficult to contain it. And for the first time in my life, it's my own future that I see. I know exactly what I have to do and defeat is not allowed.

I rush out of the house and i am stopped by Sean in my race. He returned to human form to take me in his arms.

— Go inside Sevana, it's too dangerous.

— Let me pass. I know what I'm doing.

The lion tries to hold me by the elbow, but withdraws its hand as if it had been burned.

— Sevana, you're boiling.

— Everything is fine. Don't touch me and stay behind me.

Sean does not discuss anymore and does so, even if he shifts slightly to the side so that he can observe his comrades and intervene if necessary.

I absolutely have to warn others about what is going to happen, even if I do not know exactly what will happen. So I send thoughts to them, I don't know how. I've never done this before. I'm a prophetess, not a telepath. "Put yourselves in a ball and don't move anymore". I hope they heard me. I see them looking towards me in a beautiful set, a gleam of astonishment in the bottom of their wild eyes, and obey without arguing, proof that I have succeeded. Their confident looks warm my heart. Only Connor hesitates for a second, until his gaze settles on Sean by my side. Our enemies seem confused by their reaction and find it difficult to follow this new fact. Our attackers have difficulties to inflict fatal injuries when all vulnerable parts are inaccessible.

My hands start to swarm and when I raise them in front of me, all the enemy wolves in front of my eyes literally take off from the ground. A wind of panic blows among the members of the Black pack who are struggling and fidgeting, but the grip that I have on them is intangible, to their great misfortune. In turn to be defenseless against an enemy more powerful than them. A simple gesture of the hand projects them violently against the trees, making them crack in a sinister noise. Or is it the bones of my enemies that break under the violence of the shock? Whatever. It is imperative that my new family be safe and I would have no mercy. I am a guardian angel too. A guardian angel in a mad rage that we attack her own. I shake them in all directions and hit them several times on the ground thanks to my new telekinesis talent. Sean had told me that my prediction talent would grow, he could have warned me that others would appear. Maybe he didn't know. I repeat my movements until no more than one of our attackers moves. This outpouring of power exhausted me and I feel Sean catching me when my legs no longer support me and I collapse, unconscious.

Chapter 15

Connor

Sevana has already been sleeping deeply for two days. My wounds and those of my pack members, although impressive, have all gone, while my wife does not open her eyes. When I think back to recent events, I find it hard to believe. My prophetess with embryonic talent has proven to be much more than that. It's better for me to never upset her or I might regret it. Liam has a theory about the appearance of her new powers. My soul mate is much more unique than we thought. An extraordinary fatel.

— Any signs of awakening?

— No, still nothing. Are you sure she doesn't need to go to the hospital?

— Certain. She is fine. Her body just drew on too much energy. Give her time to recover. Go release your cheetah, it will go crazy waiting, and you too.

— I don't want to leave her alone. She might need me. She will, once again, wake up in an unknown place.

— Go ahead, I'm staying with her. And don't come back before an hour or I kick your hairy ass.

I laugh when I get out of my room. Liam is right, my animal is going around in circles as if it were in a cage. Having it out in the air will help it to calm down and I know Sevana is safe in my home.

Sevana

Damn, why can't I wake up like the sleeping beauty, fresh and ready? No, I wake up constantly with aches, a clogged throat and glued eyes. And again, in a foreign bed.

— Don't move Sevana, I'm bringing you water.

I didn’t expect to find Liam by my bedside. Where's Connor? I know he's alive, I still feel our connection. He is also stressed, upset and worried.

— Where's Connor?

— Go run. He needed to unwind.

After drinking, I force myself to open my eyes and look around. I am in an undeniably masculine room. A large wooden bed and matching storage, oak parquet floors and no wall decoration. Liam, who is looking at me with curiosity, answers my silent question.

— We're at Connor's home , in the territory of the pack.

I am confused. I remember the battle, but afterwards it’s the black hole. I pay more attention to Liam and see no injuries. Besides, I no longer feel any pain.

— Did I miss another whole week of my life?

He laughs before answering me.

— No, only two days. How do you feel ?

— Extremely good indeed.

— You have no more wounds and no scars. You are like new.

— How is it possible ? Did you give me gene therapy treatment?

— No. This is due to the bond of union. Well I think. To our knowledge, there has never been a shapeshifter / fatel couple. Now, if the fatel blood strengthens our animals, it seems that the union strengthens the fatel ones. You healed at the same speed as us, as for your new talent…

— I remember. Isn't it normal to have multiple powers for a fatel? I was a little scary, right?

— Um, slightly yes. But above all you saved us. I think that the fatels do indeed all have several powers in them, but that some are dormant. The union link allowed you to activate them. This is only a hypothesis, of course. We could confirm it if there were other fatels, but … no need to say more. Chances are rare that other survivors like me exist. That doesn't stop me from hoping for it. After all, why should I be the only survivor? Other fatels may be hidden from everyone's eyes among humans as I was myself.

— I have to go. Connor arrives. Go slowly with physical exercise.

He goes out on his last words and I am peony red when Connor enters the room and hugs me.

— You scared me sweetie.

— I'm sorry, but I would never have hurt you with my powers.

— What ??? But no. I was scared when I saw you pass out. Your powers are a blessing. I know you will never be defenseless again. I would almost pity the person who tries to attack you. I told you, you're perfect.

I dive into his magnificent eyes and see his cheetah at the bottom of his irises. He then plunges his tongue into my mouth and I forget my name under his delicious caresses.

— I will never let you leave from here. You're part of the Guardian Angels pack now.

I have no problem with that. On one condition, however. Even if it means being healed…

— On the condition that wc seal our union as it should be.

That’s what we did during the next hour. And the ones after ...

Epilogue

Connor

A question has been bothering me for several days. I have to find out.

— Have you never told anyone about your talent before?

— No never. My parents had forbidden me.

— Not even your best friend? Your colleague at the hospital.

— Ashley? No, I told you, she didn't know. Why this question ? I'm safe in the pack's territory and the members all accepted me, I think. What are you afraid of?

— They all adore you. It's just that I think back to the day I asked her about you. She hesitated to tell me that you had intuition. She even wanted to hide it from me. And before revealing it to me, she asked me if I was ready to protect you, no matter who you were.

— Do you think she guessed?

— I do not know. But if it does, shc may be in danger.

END

Volume 2: Sean

The Guardian Angels pack

I have to get active. I welcome a new nurse today and have been designated to teach her everything. I guess there will have some work to make her fully operational. I have been warned that she is just twenty, so she is an inexperienced novice. She is the age I was when I started this job almost 10 years ago, and I remember very well the obstacles I had to overcome to survive. The days are not always easy to live in this profession.

Damn, I'm a little late, Peter wanted to talk to me before I leave for work. He's the alpha of the Treat pack and my dad. Well, not really, but it's just like. I owe him a lot so when he summons me, whatever the reason, I obey without arguing, like everyone else. He wanted to tell me about the new recruit at the hospital. Like most packs, we have our own geek and Peter do researches about any new people who may come near me. It is painful, but I understand the reasons. He does it for me and Sam. He protects us and I can never thank him enough for his kindness towards us. Fortunately, our conversation was quick, as she is a simple human and therefore poses no danger to us.

So I arrive with only 10 minutes of delay to the service and the new is already there, waiting quietly in the rest room for me to come and get her.

— Hello. You are Sevana, right?

— It's me. You must be the person I was told to wait here.

— Absolutely. My name is Ashley. I will be your most regular colleague on this floor and I am in charge of training you on hospital habits. I prefer to warn you right away, I can be very direct. I say everything I think without a filter, good or bad. I hope you are not susceptible.

— No problem. I prefer honesty to hypocrisy.

— Perfect. So let's go. i'm going to brief you right away, that's how we learn best. Let's start with the first bedroom. I warn you, he's a child with broken bones and lots of bruises. A bad fall on the stairs. He's in a coma, but we're expecting that he will wake up soon. You must not be too sensitive in this job or you will not last long.

— Okay. Don't worry about me. I am sure I can make myself useful.

I like her. She is a volunteer even if she seems shy.

I'm sure we'll get along well over time. I let her read the child's constants while I take the temperature. I am surprised when I raise my head. Why is she holding the boy's hand? Compassion is good, pity no. If she lets herself be overcome by her emotions, she is screwed up.

— You have to be strong, remember? I warned you.

She immediately releases his hand with a start and swings from one foot to the other, uncomfortable. I may be too abrupt. It's only her first day after all. I have been there too and I felt this sadness in front of some patients. We have to stay professional, but we are not insensitive either!

— Do you want to get some fresh air?

—No that's not it.

From the same author

Paranormal romance

Guardian Angels Series : Connor
Sean
Nate

The ottawas series: My ottawa lynx
My ottawa eagle
My ottawa beaver
My ottawa bear

The colors of the dragon

Fallen Angels Series: Dance My Angel
Run away my angel

Facebook: Viginie T.

www.ingramcontent.com/pod-product-compliance
Ingram Content Group UK Ltd.
Pitfield, Milton Keynes, MK11 3LW, UK
UKHW021933190726
13853UKWH00004B/1419

9 788835 405108